EDDIE

SPAGHETTI

EDDIE SPAGHETTI

by Edward Frascino

Harper & Row, Publishers

New York · Hagerstown · San Francisco · London

FIRST EDITION

Library of Congress Cataloging in Publication Data
Frascino, Edward.
    Eddie Spaghetti.

    SUMMARY: Ten episodes in the life of a nine-year-old
boy growing up in Yonkers during the early 1940's.
    [1. Yonkers, N.Y.—Fiction.   2. Family life—Fic-
tion]   I. Title.
PZ7.F8596Ed 1978 [Fic] 77–11850
ISBN 0–06–021908–4
ISBN 0–06–021909–2 lib. bdg.

table of contents

2174770

EDDIE

SPAGHETTI

one

THE ZOO

My name is Eddie, and I'm not fat. In fact I'm kind of thin. Skinny is more like it, but I don't mind—except when some kids, who are not my friends, call me Eddie Spaghetti. They made up this song to tease me:

Eddie Spaghetti—
Put him in a pot.
Turn on the fire
And watch him get hot.

I like to eat spaghetti. Every Sunday my mother makes it with tomato sauce and meat balls.

"Your father is getting the car out of the garage," my mother says, "and your brother is with him."

I grab my sweater out of the hall closet and put it on as I run out the front door and down the front steps.

"Take it easy," my father says. "We'll wait for you."

1

It's Sunday morning, and while my mother cooks the tomato sauce and meat balls, my father, my brother Angel, and I go to the Bronx Zoo.

Angel was seven last week and I'll be nine in November. Just two months away. My brother's name is really Angelo, but when he was a baby somebody said, "He's so beautiful. Just like a little angel." Then everybody started calling him Angel. He has dimples in his cheeks when he smiles. I wish somebody had started calling me Angel when I was a baby.

The zoo isn't far. I can tell we're there when I see the big, shiny gate my father says is made of bronze.

Some parts of the gate look like swirly trees with all different kinds of birds in the branches. There are three bronze deer over the side where the cars drive in, and three bears over the side where the cars drive out. Between the two sides is this big, swirly tree full of birds, and on top of that—at the highest place—sits a lion.

There's also a monkey and an animal that I don't recognize. I wish I could ask my father, but I'm not supposed to make him look at things while he's driving. Angel says the animal is a dog.

"Where should we go first, boys?" my father says when we get out of the car.

"The Lion House," I say.

"The seals," says Angel.

"O.K." says my father.

We have to pass the Seal Pool on the way to the Lion House, so it saves time to stop and look at the seals. The Bronx Zoo is so big, and it has so many animals, you have to stop and see the things you want to see as you come to them. Otherwise you'd do a lot of extra walking and get tired very fast.

There's a big crowd of people around the Seal Pool, so my father picks Angel up and sits him on his shoulders. Angel is smiling and his dimples show. From my father's shoulders, Angel can see over all the people's heads, but I have to squeeze through the crowd and find a place at the railing.

The seals move around a lot and bark a lot. They clap their fins together, and dive into the water and swim, and chase each other. They look like they're playing, and everybody laughs at them and has fun.

I like the seals but I don't like being crowded together with so many people. I start to squeeze my way out, backward.

"Ouch!" some lady yells when I step on her foot. "My corn!"

I didn't mean to step on anybody, but I don't apologize.

"Brat!" the lady says.

I walk over to the Lion House to see if any of the animals are in the outside cages. Empty—so I just wait in front of the Lion House for my father and Angel. I can see them from where I'm standing.

"Eddie!" My father is calling and looking all around, but he doesn't look toward the Lion House. "Eddie!"

He probably thinks I'm lost, or maybe he thinks I fell in the Seal Pool and drowned.

Angel sees me. He's telling my father and pointing to where I'm standing.

"You scared Papa," my father says to me, and he looks glad because I'm O.K. Sometimes he treats me like I was a baby.

I hold my father's hand and Angel holds his other one, and we go inside the Lion House. It smells funny but I like it. Tigers, and leopards, and cheetahs, and ocelots, panthers, and jaguars, and lynxes, and pumas all live there, too, but each one has a separate cage. Some of them walk back and forth, and back and forth, in their cages, and they look as if they really want to get out. I feel sorry for them. The lion is my favorite animal. It must be the zoo's favorite, too, because even though all those other big cats live there, the place is called the Lion House.

"Here's the big one," my father says, and we stop to look at a lion lying in his cage, licking his paw.

The lion starts to roar, and it echoes through the whole place. He looks like he would make a real nice pet. I bet if you got one when he was a little cub and raised him, he would be tame, and let you hug him, and sleep with your head resting in his mane.

"Do you want to see the snakes?" my father says.

"Yes," Angel and I say together.

Outside the Lion House my father buys us a bag of pink-and-white popcorn.

"Let me hold it," Angel says.

"You're too little," I say. "You'll spill it."

"I won't." He tries to grab the bag of popcorn.

"You will." I hold the bag over my head, and some of the popcorn spills out.

"Smarty," Angel says.

"I'll hold the popcorn," my father says, and he takes the bag from me.

Angel reaches into the bag and takes out a big handful of popcorn. He stuffs it all in his mouth. He's smiling.

"You're going to spoil your dinner," I say.

The lion is my favorite animal, but my favorite

place in the zoo is the Reptile House. It's quiet, and gloomy, and scary in here. Giant ferns hang from the ceiling, and there are palm trees painted on the walls. It's always warm, and I feel like I'm in a jungle. In the center is a huge glass cage full of rocks and tree trunks. Lying around on the rocks and tree trunks are the biggest snakes in the world. Their bodies are thick and very long. I can't tell exactly how long because they are always all curled up, and they never move.

All around in the Reptile House are smaller cages with smaller snakes, and lizards, and turtles in them. All the cages are glass because the reptiles could crawl right through a cage with bars.

We're standing in front of the cobra's cage.

"Where's the cobra?" my father asks.

"There he is," Angel says.

The cobra is all curled up under some rocks so that you almost can't see him. My father says that when a cobra gets mad he raises his head straight up and the skin behind his head spreads out like a hood. Then he bites you, and you die pretty fast. I know he can't bite me through the glass, but I wish he would open his hood.

"Sssssss!" I say real loud, but the cobra doesn't move.

I hardly ever see a snake, or a lizard or a turtle,

move in the Reptile House, and they never make a sound. If one of them ever escaped from its cage you'd never even know it, they're so quiet.

At one end of the Reptile House is a big pool where the alligators and crocodiles stay. Behind this pool are lots of real palms, and ferns, and vines, with Spanish moss hanging all around. It looks like a jungle swamp. I can't tell the alligators from the crocodiles but some of them are huge. They all have very big mouths with lots and lots of sharp teeth. Most of them are lying all on top of each other at the edge of the pool. Some are floating in the water with just their eyes and noses sticking out. They don't move either but they all look like they're smiling and waiting for somebody to fall in.

"Watch out," my father says, and he grabs Angel by his belt because Angel is standing at the railing and leaning over the Alligator Pool. I bet if he fell in those alligators and crocodiles would gobble him up in about two seconds. I throw a piece of popcorn in the water but none of them even blinks an eye.

"Can we go on the Pony Ride?" Angel asks my father.

"O.K.," my father says, "but then we have to go home. It's getting late."

When we get home, Dukie, our dog, is sitting in front of our house just like the bronze lion on the zoo's gate. Dukie barks when he sees our car, and wags his tail and jumps on my father when he gets out to open the garage door.

"Hello, Dukie," I say. "Hello, Duke."

Before Angel and I can get out of the car Dukie gets in. He's glad to see us. I bet Dukie would enjoy the zoo, but they don't allow dogs.

"The water's boiling!" my mother yells from the kitchen. "It's about time you came home. Are you ready to eat?"

She puts the spaghetti in a big pot of boiling water, and while it cooks I grate the cheese that will get sprinkled on top when it's done.

"Mario, taste the spaghetti," my mother says.

My father tastes it to make sure it's soft but not mushy.

"It's done," he says.

My mother tastes it.

"A few more minutes," she says.

"Don't cook it too long, Rose."

Most of the time we eat in the kitchen, but on Sundays, around two o'clock, we have dinner in the dining room.

Dukie sits on the floor looking up at me. He wants something to eat, too. If I feed him from my plate, he'll keep pestering me for more. So I just pat him on the head. He goes over to my mother and sits looking up at her.

"Go away, Dukie," she says. "You just had a whole can of dog food."

Dukie wags his tail and keeps looking at her. My father is smiling because he knows she can't ignore the dog. I think Dukie knows it, too.

"All right," she says. "I can't eat with you watching me."

She sticks her fork in a meat ball and takes it into the kitchen. Dukie is right behind her. She cuts the meat ball up in Dukie's dish, and when she comes back to the table she closes the kitchen door to keep Dukie in there until we finish eating. I can hear his dog license klinking against his dish while he gobbles up the meat ball.

Some Sunday I wish we would go to the zoo after dinner. Then I could sneak one of my mother's meat balls in my pocket, and when I got to the Reptile House I'd throw it in the Alligator Pool. Splash! I bet that would make those alligators and crocodiles move and snap their jaws.

two

PIANO

In her living room Grandma has a magic piano. In the top of it there's a place to put a roll of paper. The paper has a lot of small holes in it. At the bottom of the piano there are two pedals. Pumping the pedals makes the roll of paper unwind, and that makes the piano keys move down and up like magic, and it plays a song.

When we go to Grandma's on Sunday afternoon, I like to sit and pump the pedals while I move my hands over the moving keys and pretend I'm playing.

"Look at me," I say. "I'm playing."

"What a big boy!" My father smiles.

Then Angel sits next to me on the piano bench and my cousin Dotty stands behind us singing. The song is called "You Made Me Love You" and Dotty knows all the words. She knows all the words to lots of songs.

Angel's legs are too short to reach the pedals, so when it's his turn to play the piano I get down on the floor and pump for him with my hands.

Angel plays "Shine On, Harvest Moon," and Dotty sings it. Then I play "I Found a Million

Dollar Baby in the Five and Ten Cent Store" and I can sing that with Dotty because the words are printed on the roll of paper. Angel sings, too, but he can read only some of the words.

"You can read, too?" my father says to Angel. "Good boy."

After dinner one night my mother says to my father, "Mama wants to know if we want the piano. No one ever plays it anymore except when we're there on Sundays. It's just collecting dust."

"It would be nice for the children," my father says.

"Don't say yes," my mother says, "and then complain when they make noise with it."

"We'll put it in the basement," says my father. "In the playroom."

Then they start talking Albanèse. We are Italian-Albanian-Americans. My father and my mother's parents were born in a certain part of Italy that some Albanians moved to hundreds of years ago. My father and mother speak a dialect that isn't Italian and isn't Albanian—it's a mixture of both and unless a person comes from that certain part of Italy he couldn't understand it. They call the dialect Albanèse, and since I was born in the Bronx, I don't understand it.

My father and mother never taught it to Angel and me. That way they can talk Albanèse to each other when they don't want us to know what they're saying. But even though I can't understand the words, I can usually guess what they're talking about.

So now we've got Grandma's magic piano. One morning before I left for school, some men brought it in a truck and put it in our playroom. When I got home from school, I went downstairs and put on the roll that plays "I Found a Million Dollar Baby in the Five and Ten Cent Store." It feels funny having that piano in my house.

"It was a lucky April shower . . ." I start to sing, but it's no fun alone. Angel is out in the empty lot playing ball, and my mother is upstairs listening to her soap operas on the radio. I don't know why we call this the playroom—nobody ever plays here. Dukie isn't even around, but he was here earlier barking at the men who brought the piano.

"The piano came," my mother tells my father when he gets home from work.

"Good," he says. "How do you boys like your own piano?"

"It's O.K.," I say.

"It's nice," Angel says, but he hardly even looked at it.

A couple of days later I'm in the playroom playing the piano. The song is "Tea for Two," and halfway through I get tired of pumping, and I stop. I sit and look at all the little holes in the roll of paper. I bet I could make holes in a roll of paper that would play a song.

In the kitchen there's a half-used roll of paper towels that's just about the same size as a piano roll. I get it and a scissors, and start to make a piano roll of my own. Little pieces of paper are getting on the playroom floor.

When I've made holes in about four pieces of paper towel, I decide to try it on the piano. I tear off the four pieces of paper, making sure they don't tear apart, and scotch-tape one end to the end of "Tea for Two" and carefully roll it up. The other end I tape to the wind-up roll on the piano, and I start to pump.

Rip! It doesn't work.

If I only had some paper as strong as the paper in the piano rolls.

I know. I'll just make some extra holes in the "Tea for Two" roll. I untape the towel paper, and it falls on the floor. Then I take the scissors and go to work. Only it isn't work; it's play. I'm playing in the playroom.

I'm not too careful about the kind of holes I make so it isn't too long before I've made a lot of extra holes in all of "Tea for Two." I can't wait to play it.

But it sounds awful—like someone who can't play the piano very well is hitting a lot of wrong notes. When Angel comes home I'm going to ask him if he'd like to hear "Tea for Two," and when he hears how bad it sounds I'll bet he laughs.

"What's that racket?" my mother yells downstairs.

"Nothing, Ma," I yell back, and I stop pumping.

My mother comes down to the playroom, and when she sees all the paper on the floor she's mad.

"What a mess."

I just sit on the piano bench and don't say anything. Then she notices what I've done to "Tea for Two."

"What did you do?" she yells, and she hits me.

I jump off the piano bench and run upstairs.

I can hear my mother over by the washtubs now, looking for a broom and a dust pan.

"I don't have enough to do without having to clean up after you."

The washtubs are in another part of the basement, so while she's over there, I sneak downstairs, run over to the piano, and as hard as I can I hit as many keys as I can with both hands and both arms.

Brroooomplink!

16

Then I run outside through the garage so my mother can't hit me again.

"You'll get it," she yells after me.

Dukie is outside, and when he sees me running he chases after me and pulls on the bottom of my pant leg. We run through the tall grass in one of the empty lots near our house.

A lot of leaves have already fallen off the trees. I ran out so fast I didn't have time to grab my sweater. It's cold. I lie down on the ground and cover myself with dead leaves. This is fun. Like being in a big bowl of dry cornflakes. Dukie rolls around in the leaves and then comes and lies down next to me. He's nice and warm.

"I'll bet we could stay here all night, Dukie."

He wags his tail.

"But you're probably getting hungry and there's nothing here for you to eat."

He sticks his cold, wet nose in my ear. It makes me shiver.

"Come on, Dukie. We better go home so you can have your dinner."

"Those kids are starting with that piano," my mother tells my father as soon as he gets home.

"What happened?" my father says.

My mother starts talking Albanèse, and she

must be telling him about "Tea for Two."

"Eddie," my father says, "you made Mama mad."

He's very serious, and I don't know what to say—I was only trying to have some fun.

"Promise Papa that you'll play nice with the piano. You're a big boy."

"O.K."

"Tell Mama you're sorry."

"I'm sorry," I say to my mother. She looks at me as if she doesn't believe me.

"Come on," she says, "dinner's ready."

After dinner I try to make my mother laugh, so we can make up.

"Laugh," I say to my mother, and I try to look in her eyes.

"Go away," my mother says. "I'm mad at you," and she keeps her eyes on the newspaper she's reading.

"Smile," I say to my mother, and I try to put my face between her face and the newspaper.

"Don't bother me," she says, and she rattles the newspaper and looks like she's still mad, but I can tell she's ready to make up.

Then I walk out of the room and come running back in.

"Ma! Ma!" I say, like I've got something important to tell her. "Ma!"

"What's the matter?" my mother says, and she looks at me.

Now I look right in her face and I say, "Laugh."

My mother starts reading the newspaper again. She keeps her lips pressed tight together, but she almost smiled.

"Smile," I say.

"What a pest," my mother says, and she smiles just the littlest bit.

"You smiled," I say, and I watch her mouth very carefully. "Laugh."

"All right," she says, laughing.

Then I hug her, and I know she's not mad at me anymore. I feel good when I can make my mother laugh.

"Ma," I say, "can I take piano lessons?"

My mother closes her eyes and puts her hand on her forehead like she's going to faint. Then she laughs some more.

three
∫CHOOL

The alarm clock is ringing. When it stops I know that my father has turned it off and gotten up to shave, and my mother has gone downstairs to make breakfast. I pull the covers over my head and wish I didn't have to go to school.

"Get up!" my mother yells from downstairs. "You'll be late!"

I hate school. I'm checking off the days on the calendar until November eleventh, which is Armistice Day, our next holiday.

"Ma," I say when I finish my breakfast, "can I take piano lessons?"

"Don't start with that this morning," she says. "Before you leave for school make sure Dukie is in the house. I don't want him outside when the mailman comes."

"Dukie!" I call out the back door. "Here, Dukie! He's not around, Ma."

"Go or you'll be late," she says. "I'll get him in later."

Angel was ready before me this morning so he's already left. When I leave the house I see him all the way down at the bottom of the hill with his

friend Freddy. If I run I can catch up with them, but if I walk by myself and don't make too much noise I may see a rabbit. Between my house and the school there are big empty lots with tall grass and trees and bushes, and rabbits live there.

Squeak-squeak! Squeak-squeak!

The new corduroy knickers I'm wearing make squeaky sounds when one leg touches the other one. I try to walk bowlegged.

Clump! Clump! Clump! Clump!

Now my footsteps are too loud. I won't see any rabbits this morning. I hate knickers.

It isn't long before I see the top of the school sticking up over the trees. The policeman is stopping cars so Angel and Freddy and some other kids can cross the parkway. The policeman is there every morning and every afternoon because there isn't any traffic light, and cars go pretty fast on the parkway.

"Maybe he'll be sick some morning," I used to think, "and if I can't cross the parkway I'll have to turn around and go back home."

One morning he wasn't there, but they had another policeman to take his place.

I open the big, heavy door and look at the first thing you see when you walk into my school, a big clock. It's about one minute to nine so I run up the stairs as fast as I can. If I am not sitting at my

21

desk when the nine-o'clock bell rings, I am marked late. I could be inside the door of the classroom, but if I'm not at my desk, Miss Sleeper says, "You're late." She's my teacher, and she's very strict. She looks like an owl.

"Open your history books to page one hundred twenty-seven," Miss Sleeper says after she takes the role. "You look like a cow chewing on a cud, Elaine. Come up here and throw that chewing gum in the wastebasket."

After history Miss Sleeper writes some numbers on the blackboard and says, "Edward, step up to the blackboard and solve this arithmetic problem." My face always turns red when the teacher calls on me. I press hard with the chalk on the blackboard, but when I get back to my desk my numbers always look too small, and too faint and crooked, compared to the big, white, straight numbers Miss Sleeper has written. My answer is wrong, so she calls on some other kid to step up to the blackboard, and erase my answer and write the correct one. Then my face turns red again.

I misspelled two words on yesterday's spelling test, and I know what that means. I spelled "recent" r-e-c-e-i-n-t, and "license" l-i-s-c-e-n-s-e.

"Each student," Miss Sleeper says, "who misspelled two or more words on the spelling test will

remain aft⟨
misspelled ⟨
board. Rob⟨
Edward, an⟨

At three o⟨
goes home e⟨
Mary Ann, D⟨
course. Miss ⟨
thing special ⟨
home in time t⟨
can Boy on the⟨

In yesterday'⟨
paddling down⟨
kept getting str⟨
they tried to pa⟨
they saw that the⟨
waterfall. The ca⟨
over the edge wh⟨
they'll be saved. ⟨

Miss Sleeper div⟨
the seven of us. It'⟨
write one of our ⟨
times because som⟨
words and if they h⟨
five times they wou⟨
time. I have to write⟨
"I want you all," ⟨

friend Freddy. If I run I can catch up with them, but if I walk by myself and don't make too much noise I may see a rabbit. Between my house and the school there are big empty lots with tall grass and trees and bushes, and rabbits live there.

Squeak-squeak! Squeak-squeak!

The new corduroy knickers I'm wearing make squeaky sounds when one leg touches the other one. I try to walk bowlegged.

Clump! Clump! Clump! Clump!

Now my footsteps are too loud. I won't see any rabbits this morning. I hate knickers.

It isn't long before I see the top of the school sticking up over the trees. The policeman is stopping cars so Angel and Freddy and some other kids can cross the parkway. The policeman is there every morning and every afternoon because there isn't any traffic light, and cars go pretty fast on the parkway.

"Maybe he'll be sick some morning," I used to think, "and if I can't cross the parkway I'll have to turn around and go back home."

One morning he wasn't there, but they had another policeman to take his place.

I open the big, heavy door and look at the first thing you see when you walk into my school, a big clock. It's about one minute to nine so I run up the stairs as fast as I can. If I am not sitting at my desk when the nine-o'clock bell rings, I am marked late. I could be inside the door of the classroom, but if I'm not at my desk, Miss Sleeper says, "You're late." She's my teacher, and she's very strict. She looks like an owl.

"Open your history books to page one hundred twenty-seven," Miss Sleeper says after she takes the role. "You look like a cow chewing on a cud, Elaine. Come up here and throw that chewing gum in the wastebasket."

After history Miss Sleeper writes some numbers on the blackboard and says, "Edward, step up to the blackboard and solve this arithmetic problem." My face always turns red when the teacher calls on me. I press hard with the chalk on the blackboard, but when I get back to my desk my numbers always look too small, and too faint and crooked, compared to the big, white, straight numbers Miss Sleeper has written. My answer is wrong, so she calls on some other kid to step up to the blackboard, and erase my answer and write the correct one. Then my face turns red again.

I misspelled two words on yesterday's spelling test, and I know what that means. I spelled "recent" r-e-c-e-i-n-t, and "license" l-i-s-c-e-n-s-e.

"Each student," Miss Sleeper says, "who misspelled two or more words on the spelling test will remain after class, and write one of his or her misspelled words seventy-five times on the blackboard. Robert, Marilyn, Neil, Cecily, Mary Ann, Edward, and Dennis will remain after class."

At three o'clock the bell rings and everybody goes home except Robert, Marilyn, Neil, Cecily, Mary Ann, Dennis, and me, and Miss Sleeper, of course. Miss Sleeper probably doesn't have anything special to do at home, but I have to get home in time to hear *Jack Armstrong, the All-American Boy* on the radio.

In yesterday's episode Jack and his friends were paddling down a river in a canoe. The current kept getting stronger and stronger, and when they tried to paddle ashore they couldn't. Then they saw that they were coming to the top of a big waterfall. The canoe was just about to be swept over the edge when the episode ended. I know they'll be saved. But how?

Miss Sleeper divides the blackboard up among the seven of us. It's a good thing we only have to write one of our misspelled words seventy-five times because some kids misspelled five or six words and if they had to write each one seventy-five times they wouldn't get home until suppertime. I have to write "recent."

"I want you all," Miss Sleeper says, "to write

clearly and neatly. If I can't read it you'll have to do it again."

Jack Armstrong goes on at three thirty and it's already ten after.

"No talking, Neil," Miss Sleeper says. "Go to your desk and sit there until I tell you to return to the board."

Now Neil is going to be the last one to finish. Miss Sleeper is over at Neil's place at the board looking at what he has written.

"These are not clear enough, Neil." And she erases about ten of his words.

"Now," she says, "if you think you can be quiet, Neil, you may return to the blackboard."

As he picks up the chalk and starts writing again, Neil looks like he's going to cry.

Robert and Cecily are finished, and after Miss Sleeper checks their words, they go home.

Now it's twenty minutes after three and I'm finished. I'll probably miss the beginning of *Jack Armstrong*, but I'll get home in time to hear most of it.

"Miss Sleeper," I say, and my face turns red.

"Yes, Edward?" she says.

"I'm finished," I say.

Miss Sleeper takes off her glasses and wipes them with her handkerchief, and comes over to look at what I've written. She counts the "recents" to make sure there are seventy-five of them.

"Now do you know how to spell 'recent,' Edward?"

"Yes, Miss Sleeper."

"Very well. You may erase what you've written, and quietly get your coat and go home."

In the cloakroom I pull on my coat as fast as I can, and then I carefully walk through the classroom, making as little noise as possible.

"Good afternoon, Edward," Miss Sleeper says as I open the door.

"Good afternoon, Miss Sleeper."

I'm running down the hall when the classroom door slams shut.

Bang!

It sounds like an explosion because the school is so quiet.

"Edward!" Miss Sleeper sounds mad.

I'm already on the stairs but I know I'd better go back to see what she wants. I think I know. Miss Sleeper is standing in the classroom doorway looking like the biggest, meanest owl in the world.

"We do not slam the door to my classroom, Edward. Come right back inside and sit at your desk."

I hope Angel is listening to *Jack Armstrong* so he can tell me what happens. Miss Sleeper makes me sit at my desk while she checks Mary Ann's words. I've got my coat on and it's hot. Mary Ann goes home.

Now Marilyn is finished and ready to go home.

"Good afternoon, Marilyn," Miss Sleeper says.

"Good afternoon, Miss Sleeper."

"Marilyn," Miss Sleeper says, "will you show Edward the proper way to close a door?"

Marilyn looks at me like she wants to smile, but she doesn't dare with Miss Sleeper watching. Marilyn opens the door very carefully, goes out into the hall, and closes the door very carefully behind her.

"Do you think you can do that, Edward?" Miss Sleeper says.

"Yes," I say.

"Very well, you may go. Good afternoon, Edward."

"Good afternoon," I mumble.

"I didn't hear you, Edward."

"Good afternoon, Miss Sleeper," I say louder, and my face turns red.

I open the door very carefully, and go out into the hall. I close the door *very carefully* behind me. Then I stick my tongue out at Miss Sleeper through the closed door.

I run down the stairs and out of the school. I know I'll never get home in time to hear even the end of *Jack Armstrong* but I just want to get out of there as fast as I can.

After I cross the parkway, I sit down on a rock and open my English book to the last page. I draw a funny-looking owl wearing a dress. Under the owl I write "Miss Sleeper."

four
LE**ſſ**On**ſ**

"Dukie bit the mailman," my mother says when I get home from school.

Dukie jumps on me like he always does when I come home.

"He just pulls on the mailman's pant leg," I say. "He does the same thing to me when we're playing."

"He wasn't playing," my mother says. "I had to give the mailman iodine for the scratch on his leg. He said he's going to send the dog catcher here and if Dukie is running loose they'll take him to the pound."

I hug Dukie, and he licks my face.

"We'll either have to keep him tied up or put a muzzle on him."

"It isn't Dukie's fault," I say. "The mailman acts scared. That's why Dukie chases him. You're just being a good watchdog, aren't you, Dukie?"

"Tell that to the mailman," my mother says.

Poor Dukie. Being tied up is like being in a cage at the zoo.

"Ma, where's Angel?"

"At Freddy's house," she says.

That probably means he didn't listen to *Jack Armstrong*, so now I'll never know how they escaped from that waterfall.

I run past the kitchen with Dukie chasing me, and down the basement stairs to the playroom.

"Easy! Easy!" my mother yells.

I sit at the piano. Dukie lies down with his front paws around my foot and chews my shoelace that came untied.

All the piano rolls are locked up, but I can play two songs all by myself—Dotty taught me. I play "Chopsticks" and the first half of "Blue Moon." I wish I could play boogie-woogie. I wish I could play as good as my friend Dickie. He's in my class and lives across the street. Dickie has been taking piano lessons for three years, and he can play boogie-woogie and lots of things.

The oilman comes to deliver oil for the oil burner, and he has to check the gauge on the oil tank right in front of the playroom door.

"Hello, Dukie," the oilman says. "Hello, fellow."

Dukie wags his tail and goes over for a pat on the head. He likes everybody except the mailman.

I sit at the piano and play "Chopsticks" and the first half of "Blue Moon." I'll bet the oilman thinks I can play other songs, too.

"I see you got a piano," the oilman says to my mother.

"Yes," my mother says, "something new to drive me crazy."

"I know," the oilman says, smiling. "My kid takes piano lessons, too, and listening to her practice is no fun. Do you practice every day?" the oilman asks me.

"He doesn't take lessons," my mother tells him. But after the oilman leaves, I ask her, "Ma, can I take piano lessons?"

"Don't start with that piano again."

"Dickie takes lessons," I say, "and he plays good."

"Dickie practices," she says. "I'd like to see you sit and practice the piano for one hour every day."

"I'll practice. Will you ask Pa if I can take lessons?"

"I don't know," my mother says.

After dinner my mother talks to my father in Albanèse and I'm pretty sure it's about piano lessons.

"Mama says you want to learn how to play the piano," my father says to me.

"Yes."

"It looks easy," he says, "but it's hard. You have to practice every day."

"I would."

31

My father likes music, especially opera, and he's proud of Angel and me when we learn things, so I think I'm going to take piano lessons.

After Angel and I go to bed, my mother and father talk some more in Albanèse and in English.

"We'll see how much he practices," I hear my mother say just before I fall asleep.

A couple of days later I go to the school library and borrow a dog-training book. I figure I can teach Dukie to stay where he belongs so he won't have to be tied to the tree in our back yard. The rope he's tied to is long enough for him to walk around in the yard but he keeps getting it twisted around the tree.

I untie Dukie's leash from the rope. I pull up on the leash with one hand while I push down on his rear end with the other hand like it says in the book.

"Dukie, sit!" I say.

Dukie sits.

"Good boy! Good, Dukie!"

The book says to praise him and pet him when he does the right thing.

"Dukie, stay!" I start backing away from him.

As soon as I move Dukie gets up and comes with me. I get him to sit again and praise him and pet him.

"Dukie, stay!" But when I back away he comes with me.

The book says to have patience and keep repeating the command until he does it. Every time I start to back away Dukie comes with me. He wags his tail and looks like he doesn't know what's going on.

After five minutes of training the book says to let the dog rest and play with him. While we're playing I let go of his leash, and Dukie runs around to the front of the house.

"Dukie!" I yell, but now he's out in the street chasing a car. "Here, Dukie!"

The book says you're supposed to say "Come," but Dukie doesn't know that word yet.

He's across the street running toward the empty lot. He doesn't like being tied up, so now that he's loose he won't come until he's good and ready.

The car he chased passes our house. Then it stops, backs up, and parks right in front. A lady gets out. She's wearing a green hat and a fur coat, and she's carrying a leather briefcase.

"Hello there," she says. "Is this one sixty-two?"

"Yes." I hope she isn't from the dog pound. "Ma! Ma!" I yell as I run into the house.

"What's the matter?" My mother comes into the living room from the kitchen. She's wearing an apron and has a spoon in her hand.

"There's a strange lady here with a briefcase," I say.

Ding-Dong! The front doorbell.

I run down to the playroom. I hear footsteps upstairs, and voices. The lady must be in our living room. I'm glad Dukie ran away. I hope he's in a good hiding place.

"Eddie!" my mother calls. "Eddie! Where are you?"

"In the playroom!" I yell upstairs.

"Stay there. We'll be right down."

My mother and the lady come down to the playroom. The lady took off her coat but she's still wearing the green hat and carrying the briefcase. She smells too sweet and has on lots of rings and bracelets.

"This is Madam Marchisio," my mother says, "your piano teacher. She's Dickie's teacher, too."

"How do you do, Eddie," Madam Marchisio says, smiling.

"Aren't you going to say hello?" my mother says. "I told you Madam Marchisio would be here this afternoon. Did you forget?"

"Hello," I say and my face turns red. I thought she was coming tomorrow.

"Is this your piano?" Madam Marchisio says.

"I'm afraid it's kind of old," my mother says. "It belonged to my mother."

Madam Marchisio sits at the piano, takes off her rings, and begins to play. I don't recognize the song but it sounds better than the piano rolls.

"It's badly out of tune. I'll give you the name of a good piano tuner."

"Ma!" Angel yells from upstairs. "Ma!"

"Excuse me, Madam Marchisio, my other one just came in. I'm here, Angel!" And my mother goes upstairs.

"Well, my dear," Madam Marchisio says, "come and sit beside me. Have you ever studied a musical instrument?"

"No."

"Do you want to be a musician when you grow up?"

"No. I just want to play as good as Dickie."

35

"And you shall. But you must practice. Ah, music. Music. 'The universal language of mankind.'" She talks kind of fancy, like some ritzy lady in the movies.

"Do, re, mi, fa, sol, la, ti, do." Madam Marchisio sings while she plays these notes on the piano. "Do, ti, la, sol, fa, mi, re, do." That's the same thing backward.

Then Madam Marchisio sings the notes while I play them. She's nice. When I make a mistake she doesn't get mad, and when I do it right she says "Very good" and "Bravissimo!"

My first piano lesson is over. Madam Marchisio is upstairs saying good-bye to my mother, and I hear Angel coming down to the playroom.

"How was it?" he asks.

"Good. We have to get a piano tuner. Did you see all her rings?"

Angel leans against the piano.

"What did she teach you?"

I play what Madam Marchisio taught me.

"When are you going to learn boogie-woogie?"

"Probably by Christmas," I say.

I hear Dukie scratching on the back door.

"Where did you go?" my mother says when she opens the door. "Bad dog."

I run upstairs.

"Ma, you're not supposed to scold him for something he did an hour ago."

Dukie wags his tail and jumps on me.

"Good dog," I say.

Angel is downstairs playing "Chopsticks."

Every day after school I practice the piano for an hour. Then I go outside and teach Dukie to stay.

"Dukie, stay!"

I walk all the way around him in a circle, and he doesn't move.

"Bravissimo, Dukie!"

I hug him, and he licks my face.

I've been taking piano lessons for four weeks. I'm starting to learn sharps and flats, and my left hand has to play one thing while my right hand plays something else, and it all has to be in the right tempo. My father was right. It's hard to play the piano.

"Want to see what I taught Dukie to do?" I say to Angel one Saturday morning before we go to the movies.

"What?" Angel says.

"Dukie, stay!" And I walk all over the back yard. Dukie sits where I told him to stay.

"Will he do it for me?" Angel asks.

"Maybe. Stand in front of him and say 'Dukie, stay.' Then just walk away."

"Dukie, stay!" Angel says and he walks to the back door.

Dukie doesn't move.

"See?" I say.

Angel walks behind Dukie and claps his hands. Dukie looks over his shoulder but doesn't move.

Then Angel runs past Dukie and around the corner of the house. Dukie takes off after him.

Dukie stays as long as you don't run. He needs more practice.

"Eddie," Madam Marchisio says, "did you practice this week?"

"Yes," I say, and I hit another wrong note. It's dumb to lie, because she can tell whether or not I've practiced.

"I want to start you on a new piece, Eddie, but I can't until you've learned this lesson satisfactorily. I'm afraid you will have to repeat this same lesson for another week."

"O.K.," I say, even though I don't like this lesson.

"I'm not being mean, my dear. It's important to acquire a good foundation in the beginning. And to do that you must practice daily."

"I will, Madam Marchisio."

I practice the piano every day and then I make Dukie practice staying. The next time I have a lesson I play everything right.

"Very good," Madam Marchisio says. "Bravissimo!"

I'm glad that I'm getting a good foundation.

"Now I can start you on a new piece." She reaches into her briefcase and takes out some sheet music with a picture of Snow White and the

Seven Dwarfs on the cover. "Did you see *Snow White*, Eddie?"

"Yes." It was one of the best movies I ever saw.

"Then you must remember the dwarfs singing 'Heigh-Ho.' "

"I liked that," I say.

It's not boogie-woogie, but "Heigh-Ho" is a popular song. The first one she's given me. I can play it when the whole family comes to our house for Christmas dinner. I'll bet my cousin Dotty knows all the words.

It's Saturday morning, and I'm outside waiting for the mailman. Dukie is untied. The mailman just passed the Egan house at the top of the hill. He'll be here any minute. Dukie is chewing on an old bone he had buried someplace.

"Good morning," the mailman says to the lady next door.

Dukie's ears perk up.

The mailman is walking toward our house and when he sees Dukie he turns and runs.

"Dukie, stay!" I yell.

Dukie barks and takes off like a rocket.

The mailman jumps over the fence around the house next door. Dukie barks and growls and tries to jump over the fence, too. I run over and grab Dukie by the collar.

"That dog is vicious!" the mailman yells. "If

you don't keep him tied up you're going to have to pick up your mail at the post office."

I take Dukie inside our house and he runs to a window and keeps barking. My mother is outside talking to the mailman.

"Eddie," she says when she comes in with the mail, "that dog has to be kept tied up or we're going to be in trouble."

"O.K. But he doesn't have to be tied up all day, does he? Only until after the mailman comes."

"I guess that will be all right," my mother says. "But don't forget."

"You're a smart dog, Dukie, because you stay—sometimes. And if you keep practicing every day like I do I'll bet you'll stay anytime, even if a person is running. But in the meantime you have to be tied up or stay in the house until after the mailman delivers the mail." Dukie looks at me like he really understands. "That's not so bad. You can still go anyplace you want to in the afternoon. And on Sunday there isn't any mail so you can be loose all day. Come on, boy."

We go downstairs to the playroom. I sit at the piano and Dukie lies down under the piano bench.

"Heigh-Ho, Heigh-Ho, To make your troubles go . . ."

five

THE MOVIE/

"Such a beautiful day," my mother says, "and you kids are going to sit in the movies. You should be out in the sunshine."

"There'll be sunshine later, Ma," I say.

"You're ruining your eyes," she says.

"Good-bye, Ma. We're going."

Angel and I are on our way to the Central Theatre near Central Avenue, and if we walk fast we can make it in about ten minutes.

On the way we have to pass the Egan house. It's the Egan kids and their friends who call me Eddie Spaghetti. I start to get mad before I even get to their house. All the while I keep thinking, "When they see me they'll nudge each other and get ready to sing that song."

Those Egan kids are always playing in front of their house when I pass. Don't they ever play in their back yard? There they are in front of their house and they see me coming.

Eddie Spaghetti—
Put him in a pot.
Turn on the fire
And watch him get hot.

Now they're all giggling like that was the funniest thing they ever heard. I try to pretend it doesn't bother me, but it's hard to pretend you're not mad when you are.

"Come on," I say to Angel. "We'll be late." And I walk as fast as I can without running.

Even after we pass the Egan house we keep walking fast because I can't wait to get to the Central. Going to the movies is my favorite thing. I would go every day if I could, and I wouldn't even mind getting up early if instead of going to school, I could go to the movies.

On Saturdays the Central opens at a quarter to twelve but we get there about eleven thirty and wait in line with a lot of other kids. There's a clock in the box office and some kid at the front of the line keeps yelling out how much time till the doors open.

"Twelve minutes to go!" he yells.

Waiting in line is boring.

"Do you want to play Actors and Actresses?" I say to Angel.

"O.K.," Angel says.

"C.C., an actor," I say.

"Claudette Colbert," Angel says.

"No, I said an actor."

"Charlie Chaplin."

"No."

Angel stops and thinks awhile.

"Cary Grant."

"That's C.G. I said C.C."

"Seven minutes to go!" the kid at the front of the line yells.

Angel is trying to guess an actor whose initials are C.C., and there aren't many. Then I can tell by the look in his eyes that he's thought of one.

"Charles Coburn," Angel says.

"That's right," I say. "Now you give me one."

"Five minutes to go!" the kid at the head of the line yells.

"I don't want to play anymore," Angel says.

I don't either because pretty soon the cashier is going to come out and get in the box office. There she is!

Everybody cheers when the cashier comes out, and some kids start pushing—I hate that. The cashier acts like we're not even there. She's short, and old, with dyed red hair and a mean face.

I see Dickie and his little sister Adrienne.

"Hi!" Dickie says. "Can we get in front of you?"

I say, "O.K." But I don't think it's fair to the kids in line behind us.

"Hey! No sneaking in the line!" a kid behind us yells.

"Go to the end of the line!" another kid yells.

Kids start yelling and pushing. Adrienne is knocked down on her knees and starts crying.

44

Dickie starts pushing back.

"How do you like being pushed?" he says to the kid who pushed us.

"I was here first!" the kid says, and he pushes Dickie again.

"Fight! Fight!" some kid yells.

One of the ushers is coming out of the theater to see what all the noise is about. Dickie takes Adrienne's hand and they go to the end of the line.

"We'll see you inside!" I yell after them.

The cashier puts two big rolls of tickets in the ticket machine, and then she unlocks the cash box. When everything is all set up, she reaches down for her pocketbook, takes out a package of assorted candy Charms, unwraps one, and puts it in her mouth. She looks at the clock and since it isn't exactly a quarter to twelve she just sits there, sucking on a Charm, until it is. I wonder if she and Miss Sleeper are friends? At exactly a quarter to twelve the cashier starts selling tickets.

A sign in the box office says:

ADMISSION	
Adults	50¢
Children under 12	25¢

The cashier is always watching out for kids who

are twelve years old.

"How old are you?" she asks.

"Eleven and a half," a kid answers.

"When were you born?" the cashier asks.

"May 22, 1928," the kid tells her.

"You were twelve five months ago. That will be fifty cents." The kid only has a quarter so he can't go to the movies. When you lie about your age you have to lie about the year you were born, too.

There's a big kid standing behind Angel and me.

"Will you buy my ticket for me?" the big kid says to Angel.

"O.K.," Angel says, and the big kid gives him a quarter.

Then the big kid gets out of line and stands behind the box office, where the cashier can't see him.

"One child," I say and put a quarter down in front of the cashier.

She pushes a button, and a yellow ticket pops up out of a slot. I take my ticket and wait for Angel.

"Two children," Angel says to the cashier and puts down two quarters in front of her.

"Who is the other one for?" the cashier asks.

"Another child," Angel says.

The cashier is suspicious because lots of big kids ask little kids to buy their tickets for them, but

Angel looks so innocent—my mother says he could get away with murder—and he doesn't turn red like I would, so the cashier pushes the button twice, and two yellow tickets pop up.

"Thanks," the big kid says to Angel, and the three of us go in together.

Angel and I go to the candy counter. I buy Good and Plenty and Angel buys chocolate-covered peanuts.

We have to sit in the Children's Section because they think we're going to talk while the movie is on. A lot of kids do. A lady in a white uniform watches the Children's Section. She's the matron, and she has a big flashlight, and if anybody makes noise during the movie she shines her flashlight on them and says "Shhhhhhhhhhh!" Sometimes she makes more noise going "Shhhhhhhhhhh!" than the noise the kids were making in the first place. I wish I could sit in the Adult Section because I hate to miss anything the movie actors and actresses say.

When the newsreel comes on I get up to go to the bathroom.

"Save my seat," I tell Angel, and he puts his hand on the seat.

I look around, but I don't see Dickie and Adrienne anyplace.

When I get back, Angel goes to the bathroom

48

and I save his seat.

The newsreel is over and the Coming Attractions are on, and Angel isn't back yet. The movie is about to start, and he's going to miss the beginning. I turn around, looking for him, and then I see him in the aisle. He forgot what row we're sitting in, so he's walking slow and looking for me. I stand up so he'll see me.

"Down in front!" the kids behind me yell. "Sit down!"

The matron is walking up the aisle, on the other side of my row, when she hears the kids yelling. She looks over and sees me standing up, and shines her big flashlight right on me. I sit down fast and she turns off the light, but at least Angel saw me. I hope nobody saw my face turn red.

The movie is my favorite kind—a Tarzan movie. In a Tarzan movie it's always warm because it's in the jungle. The trees are big and easy to climb, and lots of shiny palm leaves and ferns grow all over. Some of the animals I see at the zoo are in Tarzan movies, but they usually get killed. I hate it when a lion gets killed.

This movie is really good, and when it ends I wish it would start again right away from the beginning.

Then a Tom and Jerry cartoon comes on and all the kids cheer. After that there's Chapter One of the new serial "Flash Gordon Conquers The Universe." It gets the biggest cheer of anything.

More Coming Attractions come on, and lots of kids get up to buy candy and go to the bathroom.

"Do you want to move to the Adult Section?" I ask Angel.

"The matron will chase us out because we're not with an adult," he says.

"Come on," I say, "and bring your coat."

I already picked out some seats next to a lady, and with all the kids running up and down the aisles, the matron won't notice Angel and me. We put our coats on the seat next to the lady, and Angel and I sit in the next two seats. The lady looks at us, and I think she smiles but it's too dark to be sure.

The second movie is a comedy with the Ritz Brothers. It takes place in a haunted house so it's funny and scary at the same time.

"Would you like a cookie?" the lady next to us says, and she holds out a box of chocolate-covered marshmallow cookies.

I'm surprised and not sure I should take one.

"I would," Angel says, and he reaches past me and takes a cookie.

They're one of my favorite kind so I take one, too. The wax paper in the box makes a loud crackling sound.

"Thank you."

"You're welcome," the lady says, and I'm pretty sure she smiled this time.

I hope the matron heard the wax paper crackle and saw the lady give us cookies, because it looks like we really are with an adult.

When something funny happens in the movie the lady laughs. She's nice. After the comedy is over, Angel and I get up to go. The lady is staying and I wish I could stay and see the Tarzan movie again with her.

"Good-bye," she says.

"Good-bye," I say.

When we get home, Angel and I act out one of the movies we've seen. We don't act the parts played by the actors; we pretend we're in the movie with the actors and have the adventures with them.

I'm captured by pygmies, who have me tied to a tree, and Angel is in the jungle looking for Tarzan. (I'm pretending to be tied to the tree in our back yard that Dukie is tied to in the morning. The empty lot next door is supposed to be the jungle.)

"Help!" I yell. "HELLLLP!"

Pygmies are all over the place piling dead branches up around my feet, and the pygmy chief is watching from his throne, and laughing.

"Help!" I yell. "HELLLLP!"

51

I try to get my hands loose but I'm tied up tight. Then drums start beating, and hundreds of pygmies are dancing around me. When the branches are piled up to my waist, the pygmy chief stands up, raises his arms, and says something in pygmy language, which is just as hard to understand as Albanèse. All of a sudden this pygmy carrying a big, blazing torch comes running toward me through the crowd. Where is Angel? This is where he and Tarzan are supposed to come in with a big herd of elephants. I knew I should have made Angel be the one who was captured.

"Help!" I yell as loud as I can. "HELLLLP!"

Instead of Angel and Tarzan, Mr. Moran, who lives up the street, comes running into our back yard.

"Did someone call for help?" Mr. Moran asks, and he really looks worried.

I turn red, and run into the house.

I go to the window and peek out through the venetian blinds. Angel runs into our back yard to rescue me from the pygmies and looks surprised to see Mr. Moran. They're talking, but I can't hear what they're saying. Then I see Mr. Moran walk away. He's smiling.

I go back outside, and Angel and I finish acting out the movie. I must be a pretty good actor if it sounded to Mr. Moran like I really needed help.

six

CHRI/TMA/ TREE

"Ma," I say the day after Thanksgiving, "can we take out the Christmas decorations?"

"It isn't even December," my mother says. "They aren't even selling trees yet."

Two weeks later I say, "They're selling trees on Yonkers Avenue, Ma. Can we get ours?"

"We'll see," she says, "if your father feels like going tonight when he gets home from work. If not, you'll have to wait until Saturday."

I hope it's tonight, because there's a good movie at the Central this Saturday.

When my father gets home, the first thing he does is give me the newspaper so I can look at the funnies to see what's happening in my favorite comic strips.

"Pa, can we get our tree tonight?" I ask. I don't sit right down on the floor and read the funnies like I usually do.

"Papa's tired tonight," my father says. "We'll go Saturday."

"But Pa, all the good trees might be sold by Saturday. Can't we go tonight? Please?"

"O.K.," he says. "But first can we eat dinner?"

53

Then I sit on the living-room floor, and read the funnies while my father washes his hands. My mother talks to my father in Albanèse, and I think she's mad because he let me have my way.

After dinner my father, Angel, Dukie, and I drive down to Yonkers Avenue to buy a Christmas tree. Before we leave the house my mother says, "You're not going to put that tree up tonight. It's late and you have school tomorrow."

The place where they sell the Christmas trees is an empty lot. Some of the trees are lying on the ground in piles, and some are standing up leaning against the building next to the empty lot. Some trees are very tall, and some are very small, and there are all sizes in between. All of them have rope wrapped around them so the branches won't stick out and break.

"Here's a nice one," says the man who sells the Christmas trees. "Nice and full."

He unwraps a big tree, and spins it around so the branches all stick out. It looks good, but it's way too tall to fit in our living room.

"Oh boy!" my father says, laughing. "Too big."

"Too big," the Christmas-tree man says. "No problem. We got all sizes."

He unwraps a shorter tree and spins it around. This one looks like it will fit in our living room, but the branches are uneven. Some of them stick out too far, and some of them don't stick out far enough.

"It's crooked," my father says.

"The trees this size are all like that," the Christmas-tree man says. "If you want it full and even all around, take the big one, and cut some off the top."

"What do you say, boys?" my father asks Angel and me,

"The big one," I say.

"I don't know," Angel says.

The big one costs $7.50 and the crooked one costs $4.00. My father buys the crooked one. The Christmas-tree man wraps the tree up again and ties it to the roof of our car. Dukie barks at him from inside.

When we get home, we leave the tree out on our front porch.

"Was it expensive?" my mother asks my father.

"Four dollars," my father tells her.

"The one last year," my mother says, "was only three."

The next afternoon my mother, Angel, and I go to the five-and-ten. We buy three boxes of tinsel and a big roll of cotton.

That night after dinner, we take the tree in from the porch. Dukie sniffs it.

"It's lopsided," my mother says when my father

unwraps the branches. "You paid four dollars for a lopsided tree. Where was your head, Mario?"

"Be nice, Rose," my father says. "We'll put the lights and the decorations on and it will look good. You'll see.

My father screws the tree stand on the bottom, and now a Christmas tree is standing in our living room.

My mother has taken out all the boxes where the decorations are kept, and she's testing the lights to be sure they work before we put them on the tree.

"I'll make the snow," I say.

While my mother and father and Angel are putting the lights on the tree, I go to the kitchen and mix Ivory Flakes with a little water until it makes a paste. I'm going to spread it on the branches to look like snow. It's an idea that I heard on a radio commercial for Ivory Flakes. Dukie is watching me. He thinks I'm making something to eat, but when I let him sniff it, he goes back into the living room.

After the lights and the snow are on, we start to hang the ornaments; but first my mother wraps the cotton around the tree stand. She doesn't like the stand to show, and the cotton is supposed to look like snow, too.

"Here's a nice one," my father says. "Eddie,

hang this in the front." And he hands me a big pink-and-white-and-green ornament. "Where's the bird?"

"Don't you remember?" my mother says. "The kids broke it last year."

Some of the ornaments are real old. We used to have a pretty one that went at the very top of the tree, but it broke, too, so we bought an angel to take its place. The angel has a white dress, and blond hair, and silver wings, and a silver halo. One of the lights is set behind her head to make the halo look like it's shining.

On the floor, in front of the tree, we put the Nativity. Inside the stable are little figures of Jesus, Mary, and Joseph, and their donkey, and a cow. My father says the cow breathed on the baby Jesus to keep him warm, so the cow is standing over the manger, and Mary and Joseph are kneeling on each side of it. On top of the stable we put an angel praying—it doesn't look like my brother—and a star. We set another light behind the star.

Now my mother and father go and do the dinner dishes, and talk Albanèse, and Angel and I start hanging the tinsel on the tree.

"You start on that side," I tell Angel, "and I'll start over here."

"O.K.," Angel says, and he yawns.

I like a lot of tinsel on the tree, but each piece

has to be hung separately so it doesn't get tangled. This takes a long time, and Angel and I are getting tired, and we have to get up for school, so we'll probably finish it tomorrow. We go upstairs to our rooms.

"It's snowing," Angel says.

"Is it sticking?" I run to his bedroom window and look out with him. "I hope it snows all night and gets so deep that tomorrow school will be closed."

"Remember the blizzard we had?" Angel says. "When there was so much snow, school was closed for two days."

"And," I say, "it was so deep it almost came to the top of the garage door. I hope this is a blizzard."

"It's late!" my mother yells from downstairs. "Go to bed, you two!"

Angel and I watch the snow for a few more minutes, and then he goes over to his bed and gets under the covers.

"Want to go sleigh riding," I say, "if there's no school tomorrow?"

"O.K." And he pulls the covers up to his chin.

I go to my room, but I don't turn on the light. I stand at my bedroom window and watch the snow some more. Everything outside is getting covered, even the clothesline. I open the window and stick out my head. The snow tickles and feels cold on my nose and ears. I open my mouth and catch some snowflakes on my tongue. It tastes good—just like snow.

It's very quiet outside, and not as cold as you'd expect. I start to feel sleepy so I pull in my head, close the window, and get into bed. As soon as I get under the covers I pull up the legs of my pajama pants. I always do that because if I don't my legs get hot during the night. I prop my pillow up against the wall so I can see out the window from bed. The snow looks nice, and I hope it's a blizzard.

In the morning everything outside is white, but it isn't snowing anymore. I take a long time to eat my breakfast, hoping the radio will say my school is closed.

"Eat," my mother says. "They haven't announced that any schools are closed."

I finish breakfast and put on my galoshes, and my sweater, and my scarf, and my coat with the hood, and my woolen gloves. School is open. Angel puts on his galoshes, and his sweater that used to be mine, and his scarf, and his coat with the hood, and his woolen gloves.

"Look at the tree," I tell Angel when we get outside. From the street in front of our house you can see the Christmas tree through the French doors.

"It looks nice," he says.

We start off down the hill to school, and we're the first ones to make footprints in the snow. I like walking in snow but I wish I wasn't walking to school.

When I get there the cloakroom looks like the Great Lakes with all the wet galoshes making puddles on the floor. Five kids are absent.

"It seems," Miss Sleeper says, "that some students are afraid of a little snow." And she sneezes. "Excuse me," she says, and blows her nose.

Miss Sleeper's nose is red and she looks like she has a cold, but she would never be absent. If it had been a blizzard, she probably would be the only one in the whole school.

Yesterday we had a long hard English test, and now Miss Sleeper is returning the test papers. Everybody gets theirs except me.

"One test paper is perfect," Miss Sleeper says. The classroom is very quiet. "Edward, you may come up and get your paper."

I'm glad I got a hundred percent, but I hate that my face turns red when I go up for my paper.

"Nice work, Edward," Miss Sleeper says, and she's smiling.

"Thank you, Miss Sleeper." I try not to run back to my desk.

At lunchtime the lunchroom is crowded. A lot of kids who usually go home for lunch brought their lunch today because of the snow. Angel and Freddy and Dickie and I eat together.

In the afternoon we do reading and geography. I wish I was outside making a snowman, or having a snowball fight, or sleigh riding. And I also have to finish putting the tinsel on the Christmas tree. Finally it's three o'clock.

The Great Lakes in the cloakroom have dried up. I put on all my stuff and go out in the snow again. On the way home I try to find the footprints I made this morning, but it's not easy because other people have made footprints since then.

When I get home, I take off all my stuff and go to the living room to put the rest of the tinsel on the tree, but it's already done. My mother did it while Angel and I were at school.

Now I can go sleigh riding down the big hill in front of my house. It's perfect because hardly any cars ever come by. I put on my galoshes, sweater, scarf, coat, and gloves.

"Eddie!" my mother yells from upstairs. "Before you go anywhere, shovel some snow!"

I pretend I didn't hear, and go down to the garage and get my sled. Angel is over at the

Kramer kids' house having a snowball fight, and nobody else is sleigh riding, so I have the hill all to myself. Hooray!

I hold my sled up in front of me and run a few steps to get started, then I dive forward with the sled under me, and when the sled hits the snow I start gliding down the hill faster and faster. Snow is blowing in my face and it feels good. At the bottom of the hill I have to turn left or else I'll crash into a snowbank. By the time I get near the bottom I'm going real fast, and I have to start turning gradually because if I make it too sharp I'll turn upside down with the sled on top of me. I make a good turn, and then I start to slow down until I stop. The street I turn into is flat as a pancake.

Now comes the part I hate about sleigh riding—I have to pull my sled all the way back up to the top of the hill. When I get to the top again Adrienne is coming out of her house with her sled. She's even littler than Angel, and I hope she doesn't get in my way.

"Hi, Eddie."

"Hi."

Adrienne lies face down on her sled and uses her hands to push herself along until she starts gliding. She looks like she's swimming.

"Want a push?"

"O.K."

I give her a push and she's on her way. I watch her gliding down the hill faster and faster. When she gets near the bottom, she starts to turn left, and almost turns upside down but she doesn't.

After I see her turn the corner into the flat street I start down the hill. I'm going great, and I hope when I turn into the flat street Adrienne isn't standing in my path. If I have to swerve around her I could lose my balance and turn upside down.

I'm turning fine now. Then I slow down on the flat street until I stop.

"It's mine!" Adrienne is saying, and she's crying.

This big kid in a plaid jacket is trying to take her sled. Adrienne is sitting on her sled and the big kid is pulling on the rope tied to the steering bar. He pulls straight up, and Adrienne slides off the back into the snow. She starts crying louder.

The big kid doesn't say anything. He gives me a mean look and starts to walk past me, pulling Adrienne's sled behind him. I feel sorry for Adrienne. I don't know what else to do so I pick up this big piece of frozen snow and hit the big kid over the head with it. He's taller than me so I really have to stretch to reach his head.

The piece of frozen snow breaks into a lot of

smaller pieces, and it doesn't seem to hurt him at all. The big kid is surprised for a second and then he's mad. He pushes me down and pins my arms under his knees. I kick and squirm but I can't get away. He picks up a big handful of snow and rubs it in my face. I try to turn my head away and my hood comes off, and snow gets in my ear, and under my scarf, and down my back. It feels awful.

All of a sudden the big kid gets off me and looks around. I guess he's looking for Adrienne's sled, but it's gone and so is Adrienne. My sled is gone, too.

I sit up and wipe the snow off my face. The big kid looks at me, and I think he's going to rub more snow in my face and beat me up, but he just kicks some snow at me and walks away with his hands in his pockets.

I get up and my scarf is kind of soggy. Some snow got down inside one of my galoshes, but I'm O.K. When I get to the bottom of the hill, I see Adrienne almost at the top pulling both sleds behind her.

"Thanks, Eddie," Adrienne says when I get to the top of the hill. Her nose is running.

"That's O.K.," I say. "You were smart to take my sled, too. Thanks."

"'Bye." Adrienne walks toward her house.

"'Bye."

"Your tree looks nice," Adrienne yells across the street.

"Thanks."

I take my sled into the garage and get a snow shovel. I shovel a narrow path from the front door, down the steps, and all the way to the sidewalk in front of my house. It makes me tired so I go inside.

I can't wait for it to get dark. I like to turn out all the lights except the lights on the Christmas tree, and just sit on the floor and look at how everything on the tree shines and sparkles. My father gets mad when we leave a lot of lights on in the house, so besides looking nice, it saves electricity.

It's dark when my father gets home. Everything outside is covered with snow, and inside only the tree lights are on.

"It looks nice, my big boy," my father says to me. He's smiling a big smile, and the tip of his nose is red from the cold. "You want the funnies?" And he hands me the newspaper. Then he takes off his hat and coat, and puts them in the hall closet.

I slide over as close to the tree as I can so I can read the funnies by the lights. I can't wait until Christmas, when all the presents will be right where I am now. I wonder what I'm going to get.

seven

SCISSORS

"Can I have the scissors?" Angel asks.

"I'm not finished yet," I say.

I'm cutting heads out of the Sunday funnies. I have a good head of Dick Tracy, without his hat on, that I'm going to paste on a piece of drawing paper, and then I'm going to draw a Tarzan body under it. I think I'll make him swinging on a vine, and if it turns out good I'm going to hang it up.

I can draw heads but for this drawing the faces have to have the right expressions, and I can't draw expressions as good as the ones in the funnies. While I'm looking for a girl's head for this drawing, I'm cutting out other heads I like and saving them. I may paste a lot of them on one piece of paper and make them all cowboys and Indians, or people in old-fashioned costumes. It's best to use the Sunday funnies because they are in color and then I can color the bodies I draw with the paint set Dotty gave me for Christmas.

"Are you finished yet?"

"No," I say. "Can't you use the other scissors?"

"They're too big."

I'm using the small pair of scissors my mother uses for sewing.

"What are you making?" Angel says. "Paper dolls?"

"No."

"Well, how much longer is it going to take?"

"I don't know."

It's not easy cutting heads out of the funnies. You have to be very careful and cut close so you don't get any background, but not too close or you may cut off some hair, or a chin, or an ear.

"Finished?"

"Not yet." I wish he would stop pestering me.

Now he's standing right next to me, watching. I'm cutting a girl's head out of *Terry and the Pirates* to be Jane in my Tarzan drawing. She looks pretty and frightened. She's going to be in a river with a crocodile after her, and Tarzan will be swinging down to save her.

"What are you going to do with all these heads?" Angel says, and he picks one up.

"Don't mix them up."

"Well, what are you going to make?"

"Drawings."

"Drawings of what?"

"Drawings of different things," I say. "I can't tell you about them now. Stop pestering me."

All he ever draws is fire engines, fire engines, and more fire engines. And he shows them to everybody like they were the greatest drawings in the world.

"Angel is going to be an artist when he grows up," people are always saying.

He draws pretty good fire engines, but with all the practice he gets they should be good.

"Come on," Angel says, "I only need the scissors for a minute."

"Well you can't have them!"

"I'm going to tell Ma you're hogging the scissors," he says. "Ma!" Angel yells, and he starts to leave my room. "Ma!"

"Now look what you made me do." My hand slipped and I cut off the top of the girl's head. "Here!" I yell. "Take the old scissors!" And I throw them at him.

The scissors hit the wall and fall on the floor. I didn't aim to hit him. Even if I had, I probably would have missed. My aim is awful.

"Dummy!" Angel yells. He picks up the scissors and throws them back at me.

I feel a sting under my left eye.

"Oh my God!" my mother says. She came into the room just as Angel threw the scissors.

I've got one hand over my eye, and blood is running down my face. My mother rushes over to me and pushes my hand away.

"Let me see!" she says. "Thank God it's not the eye. Come." And she leads me out of my room.

Angel is standing in the doorway looking very scared.

"Are you crazy?" my mother says to him. "You could have blinded your brother." And she slaps Angel on the side of his head.

Angel starts to cry, and he runs downstairs.

My mother takes me into the bathroom. She wets a washcloth and puts it over the cut.

"Hold that," she says to me.

She opens the medicine cabinet and takes out cotton, gauze, adhesive tape, peroxide, and iodine.

"Not iodine, Ma!" I yell. I hate iodine. It stings.

She takes the washcloth away and looks at the cut.

"Still bleeding," she says, and she presses the washcloth against my face and holds it tight.

When the bleeding finally stops, my mother cleans around the cut with peroxide. I know what's coming next. Iodine.

"Ooooooooo!" I yell, and I turn around in a circle shaking my head. The iodine hurts worse than the scissors did. I don't see how something that feels so awful can be good for a person.

My mother makes a bandage that goes all around my head. To cut the gauze and adhesive tape she uses the same scissors that Angel and I were fighting over. I see myself in the mirror on the medicine cabinet. I look like a wounded soldier. My mother takes me back to my bedroom and makes me lie down.

"Stay quiet," she says, "or you'll start bleeding again. What happened? Why did Angel throw the scissors at you?"

"I don't know."

My mother looks at me. Then she walks out of my room, closes the door, and goes downstairs. She's probably going to find Angel. I'll bet he's hiding.

Whenever Angel does something bad, I always get blamed for putting him up to it. My mother calls me "the instigator."

I hear my mother yelling downstairs. I get up off the bed and open the door a little to try and listen.

"He threw them at me first!" I hear Angel yell.

Someone is coming upstairs, so I quickly close the door and jump back on the bed. I hear my door open but I can't see who it is because my eyes are closed. I'm pretending to be asleep, but I feel my eyelids moving.

"Open your eyes," my mother says. "I know you're not asleep."

I open my eyes very slowly and look up at my mother.

"I want to get to the bottom of this," she says.

"Angel keeps saying that you threw the scissors at him first. Is that true?"

"My face hurts," I say, and it does. "Is it bleeding again?"

"You're not bleeding," my mother says, "and more than your face is going to hurt if you don't tell me the truth. Did you throw the scissors at your brother first?"

"He was pestering me," I say, "and he made me ruin something I was cutting out."

"So you threw the scissors at him," my mother says.

"Yes," I say, "but I didn't hit him."

"That's beside the point," my mother says. "You might have hit him. What Angel did was wrong. But I don't think he would have thrown the scissors if you hadn't thrown them at him first."

That's what I mean. Angel just almost blinded me and I'm getting blamed for it.

"You did a bad thing," my mother says, "and you were punished for it. I hope you've learned your lesson. Now I want you to rest until suppertime." And she goes downstairs.

The heads I cut out are all over the floor and there's blood on my drawing pad. I wonder what Angel needed those scissors for in the first place. He never said.

I take my shoes off and tiptoe to the bathroom.

There on the side of the bathtub, right where she left them, are my mother's little sewing scissors. I pick them up and tiptoe back to my room.

I start looking through the Sunday funnies again. I have to find a pretty and frightened girl's head to be Jane in my Tarzan drawing.

eight
JUVENILE DELINQUENCY

"Do you want to see a picture of a naked man and a naked woman?" my friend Neil says.

"O.K.," I say.

I'm over at Neil's house, and his mother isn't home. She's a nurse, and she has all these medical books in a bookcase with glass doors. The bookcase is locked but Neil knows where his mother keeps the key. He unlocks the bookcase and takes out a big, thick book with a green cover.

Neil opens the book and giggles. On one page there's a picture of a naked man and on the other page there's a picture of a naked woman. The pictures are on flaps and in color. When you lift the flaps you see the inside of a person's body on more flaps. The muscles are on the first flap under the skin, and under that is another flap with the skeleton on it. Under that, on the page itself, is the brain, and the heart, and the liver, and the lungs, and the intestines, and all that stuff. It's a pretty interesting picture.

The back door slams, and Neil closes the book so fast he nearly tears one of the flaps.

"Hi," Gloria says as she comes into the room.

Neil is just locking the door to the bookcase.

"Hi, Gloria," he says.

Gloria is Neil's sister, and she's a year younger than us.

"What are you doing in Mommy's bookcase?" Gloria says.

"Nothing."

"Mommy's going to be mad if you were fooling around with her medical books."

"I didn't hurt anything. I was just showing Eddie some pictures."

"I bet I know which picture."

"Mommy's going to be mad," Neil says, "when she finds out you were playing with her lipstick."

Gloria's mouth is covered with lipstick. It goes all the way up to her nose.

"I wasn't playing with Mommy's lipstick. This is my lipstick." And she takes out a lipstick and puts on some more.

"Where did you get lipstick?"

"In the five-and-ten."

"You don't have any money," Neil says. "How could you buy lipstick?"

"I didn't. I took it."

"You're a thief!" Neil says. "If they find out, you'll go to reform school."

"The five-and-ten has lots of lipstick," Gloria says. "They won't miss just one, and anyway, nobody saw me. It was easy. If you weren't such a sissy you'd have taken that harmonica instead of saving up your allowance for two weeks to buy one."

"I'm going to tell Mommy."

"If you do," Gloria says, "I'll tell her that you know where she keeps the key to her bookcase. I'll tell her you traced pictures out of her medical book."

"I have to go home," I say to Neil. "Good-bye."

"You're a liar, Gloria!" I hear Neil yelling as I go outside. "You're a juvenile delinquent!"

On my way home I'm wondering if it's really that easy to take things from the five-and-ten. My mother usually buys me anything I want, but I just wonder how a person gets away with stealing something.

A few days later in school, Cynthia's fountain pen is missing. Miss Sleeper finds it in Robert's desk. Robert wasn't going to keep the pen. He was mad at Cynthia and he just wanted to tease her. But you can imagine how mad Miss Sleeper is at Robert. She's making his mother come to school. Some kids say he might get expelled. What I can't figure out is *when* Robert took Cynthia's pen. Nobody saw him.

I would never take anything that belonged to

somebody else, but like Gloria said, "The five-and-ten has lots of lipstick. They won't miss just one." The five-and-ten has lots of a lot of things.

When Angel and I come out of the Central Theatre on Saturday, Angel starts walking toward home.

"Wait a minute," I say. "Ma gave me money to buy Scotch tape. We have to go to the five-and-ten."

"I want to go home," Angel says. "I'm going over to play at Freddy's house."

"Come with me. It won't take long."

"No. I told Freddy I'd come over as soon as I got home from the movies. I'm going."

"You can't cross Yonkers Avenue by yourself."

"I can cross," Angel says, and he starts to walk to the corner.

"Wait for the light!" I yell after him.

I watch Angel until he gets to the corner. The light is red. He waits for it to turn green, he looks both ways, and then he crosses Yonkers Avenue. My brother gets smarter every day, and pretty soon he'll be able to do everything I can do.

The five-and-ten is right near the Central.

The first counter inside is the cosmetics counter. There's cold cream, and hair dye, and nail polish, and nail-polish remover, and mascara, and powder, and rouge, and lipstick. Gloria sure has a lot of nerve taking something from a counter right in the front of the store. The lady behind the counter has on a brown smock. She doesn't look like you could get away with taking anything from her counter.

I like the toy counter, so I walk back there to see if they have anything new. They have lots of little lead soldiers, and cowboys, and Indians. One of the Indians looks just like an Indian I used to have, but then I lost him.

There are some new yo-yos, too. I pick one up, and try it. It works real easy—not like the one I have at home, which is old and has a knot in its string. The lady behind the toy counter is watching me. I put the yo-yo back and I notice some harmonicas. I wonder if they're like the one Neil bought?

On the way over to the stationery counter to buy the Scotch tape, I have to pass the notions counter where they have needles, and pins, and ribbons, and lots of spools of thread, and lots and lots of buttons. Some of the buttons are little, white shirt buttons, and some are big, round coat buttons. They are all different colors and sizes, and they're all attached with thread to small, flat pieces of cardboard.

The clerk behind the notions counter is giving

change to a lady, and another lady is looking through the spools of thread. I pick up a card with buttons on it and put it in my coat pocket. I don't even know what kind of buttons I took, but I hope nobody saw me.

I keep my hand in my pocket. I can feel the buttons—there are six of them. Then I take my hand out of my pocket because I think that looks suspicious.

When I get to the stationery counter, I pick up a roll of Scotch tape and hand it to the lady behind the counter.

"Sixteen cents," the lady says.

The money my mother gave me is in the same pocket as the buttons. I'm afraid the buttons might fall out when I take out the money. The lady is looking at me. She put the Scotch tape in a bag and she's holding it, waiting for me to pay. My face starts to turn red.

I feel a dime, and then I feel another one. I'm very careful when I take the dimes out of my pocket. But I'm sure a corner of the cardboard must be sticking out.

I hand the lady the two dimes. She punches some keys on the cash register, puts the dimes in, takes out four pennies, and hands them to me with the bag. I put the pennies in my pocket, and

push the card with the buttons in as far as it will go.

As I walk out of the store, the lady in the brown smock is talking to the manager. She looks at me when I pass her counter. Did she see me take the buttons? Is she telling the manager?

I'm out on the street, and I expect him to come running after me. I want to turn around but I'm afraid. I want to run but that would really be suspicious. When I get to the corner I have to wait for the light. It turns green, and I run across Yonkers Avenue, and I keep running up the other side of the street.

"Did you get the Scotch tape?" my mother says when I get home.

"Yes," I say, and I put the tape and the four pennies on the dining-room table.

Dukie jumps on me and wags his tail. I keep my coat on and go right up to my room. Dukie comes with me. I close the door and take the cardboard out of my pocket. Dukie sniffs it. Attached to the cardboard are six shiny red buttons about the size of nickels, and printed on the cardboard is: La Mode, #104, 19¢.

"Dukie, I'm a thief."

I saw a movie once where a very poor man stole a loaf of bread because his family was hungry. At least he had a good reason for stealing. Even

Gloria stole something she wanted to use. But what am I going to do with six red buttons? The first thing I have to do is hide them.

Where?

In my bottom drawer under my sweaters. No. My mother might take my sweaters out to wash them.

Under my mattress—between the mattress and the bedspring. No. My mother turns my mattress upside down sometimes when she cleans.

I have to hide the buttons someplace where nobody looks but me. I know. My pile of comic books in the corner. Nobody looks there—not even Angel unless he asks first.

I take Dukie out in the hall and quickly go back into my room and close the door. He's scratching on the outside of my door and whining. I put the buttons between two comic books, and put a lot of other comic books on top.

That night when my father comes home he gives me the funnies, and I sit on the floor and read them. I hope he never finds out that I'm a thief. He wouldn't say "Good boy" to me anymore.

The first half of the school term is almost over. We're going to elect a new Class President, Vice-President, Secretary, and Treasurer.

Yesterday Dickie nominated me for Class Treasurer. Geraldine Prang seconded the nomination. Milton Bressler is the other candidate for Treasurer. He's one of the smartest kids in the class, so he'll probably win.

Anyway, I have to write a campaign speech. It's going to be short and at the end I'm going to say, "My actions will speak louder than words." Stealing from the five-and-ten sure speaks louder than words. Nobody would trust a thief to be Class Treasurer. And how would Dickie and Geraldine feel if they knew? They nominated me.

After dinner I go downstairs and practice the piano. My mother and father and Angel are in the living room listening to the radio.

"You want to hear *Lux Radio Theatre?*" Angel yells down to me. "It's good!"

"I have to practice!" I yell back. I want to be good and practice for a whole hour.

"My mother," Neil tells me the next day, "found out about Gloria stealing the lipstick."

"How did she find out?"

"I don't know," Neil says.

I'll bet he told on his sister.

"What happened?" I say.

"Well," Neil says, "first Gloria got spanked, and then my mother took her to the five-and-ten.

She couldn't give the lipstick back because she used some, but my mother made Gloria tell the manager that she stole the lipstick. Then she had to pay for it, and say she was sorry, and promise never to steal anything ever again. Now Gloria doesn't get any allowance, and she can't go to the movies for a whole month. Everybody at the five-and-ten knows she's a thief, so she can't go there anymore either."

I wish I could tell somebody besides Dukie about the buttons but it wouldn't be Neil. He can't keep a secret. I wonder if my mother would do what Gloria's mother did. I know my mother would be mad. I wish I hadn't taken those dumb buttons. Maybe I should throw them away or burn them.

It doesn't matter what I do with them. I'm still a thief as long as I stole them from the five-and-ten. But nobody saw me. Maybe I could put them back without anybody seeing me again. That's what I'll do. I guess I'll never be a juvenile delinquent because my conscience bothers me too much.

Today is the day.

I take the buttons out of their hiding place, and with a handkerchief I very carefully wipe each button and both sides of the cardboard so there won't be any fingerprints. Now that all my old fingerprints are wiped off, I have to be careful not to make new fingerprints, so I put on my gloves. I put the buttons in my coat pocket and go downstairs.

"I'm going out to play, Ma!" I yell before I go out the front door.

"Want to play catch?" Angel asks. He's sitting on the front steps holding a baseball in his catcher's mitt.

"When I get back," I say.

"Where are you going?"

"To the store."

"I'll walk with you."

"No! It'll be faster if I go alone. I'll be right back."

I look over my shoulder a few times to make sure Angel isn't following me.

I don't see the manager anyplace in the five-and-ten when I get there, and the lady in the brown smock isn't at the cosmetics counter. This is going to be easy.

I head for the notions counter, but I make a quick turn toward the toy counter. My heart feels like it just jumped into my throat. The lady in the brown smock is working behind the notions counter, and nobody is over there buying anything. I walk around the toy counter twice, but I

86

don't pick anything up because I might drop it with my gloves on. Wool gloves are slippery.

I wouldn't dare try putting the buttons back right in front of the lady in the brown smock, so I guess I'll have to come back another day when she's working at a different counter.

Then I see a customer over at the notions counter buying things. I'll bet I could put the buttons back while the lady in the brown smock is busy at the cash register. I walk over, and slow down when I get to the place where all the buttons are.

I stop and pretend that I'm looking at buttons. I hear the cash register ring, and I know the lady in the brown smock must be getting change. I start to take the buttons out of my pocket but one of the corners of the cardboard is stuck. The corner bends as I yank the cardboard out, and then I drop it on the floor!

I bend down to pick up the buttons but I can't with my dumb wool gloves on. I should have thrown the buttons away. It was easier being dishonest than it is being honest.

Finally I get hold of the buttons, and I bend the cardboard some more. Then I put them back with all the other red buttons.

"Hey!" the lady in the brown smock yells at me.

Maybe I could run for it, but now the manager

is standing near the door. The lady in the brown smock is standing right across the counter from me.

"Sonny," she says, "take your gloves off before you handle the merchandise. What do you want?"

"Nothing," I mumble, and my face turns redder than the buttons I just put back.

As I walk away I hear her say, "These kids," while she straightens up the buttons. I wonder if she notices that one of the cardboards is bent, but it doesn't have my fingerprints on it.

What a relief!

When I get outside I feel great, and I'll never, as long as I live, ever steal anything again. Not even a loaf of bread if I'm starving to death.

We've finished our midterm tests in school. Today is Election Day for the new class officers.

"Edward," Miss Sleeper says, "step up to the front of the room and give your campaign speech. And speak up so I can hear you." She's standing all the way in the back of the room.

When I stand up in front of the class my face turns red. I'm the last nominee to give a speech. After I finish we have the election. I don't know whether to vote for myself (would that be stuck up?) or for Milton Bressler. I decide it wouldn't be stuck up so I vote for myself.

After Robert, Cynthia, Marilyn, and Dickie

count the votes, Miss Sleeper announces the winners.

"And for Class Treasurer, Milton Bressler."

Just as I expected.

"You only lost by five votes," Dickie tells me after school.

I guess a lot of the kids would trust me enough to be Class Treasurer.

nine
POIƧON IVY

"Don't scratch," my mother says. "You'll spread it."

She's putting calamine lotion on my face so it won't itch so much. I've got poison ivy, and my face is all swollen and covered with a rash. My eyes are swollen so bad they look like little slits. It's like I'm living in a horror picture where the mad doctor mixes a potion that bubbles and smokes, and drinks it, and turns into a monster. I look like a monster, and I'd like to sneak over to the Egan kids' house. I'd like them to see me looking in their window while they're listening to something scary on the radio like *Lights Out* or *Inner Sanctum.*

It's really hot today and it has been all week—the radio says it's a heat wave.

I'm itchy—don't scratch.

Angel went swimming at Tibbetts Brook Park swimming pool but I couldn't go because of this dumb poison ivy. During summer vacation Angel and I go swimming at Tibbetts every nice day, and sometimes on Sundays my father takes us to Jones

Beach instead of to Grandma's.

I just had a terrible itching attack, but I didn't scratch.

I like the summer because it's warm all the time, and you can go outside without a coat, even at night when the fireflies are out. During the day I like to play in the woods. All the leaves are out on the trees and in some places only little spots of sun shine through, and everything smells so good. It's easy to pretend that I'm in a jungle. I wish I could go barefoot like Tarzan, but the bottoms of my feet are too soft, and there are lots of sharp stones and prickly things on the ground.

There's also poison ivy. I know all the spots where it grows and I keep away from them. But no matter how careful I am, I always get it once every summer.

I can't help it, I have to scratch this second. That felt good, but now it's itching worse.

My mother says to try to think of something else, but the only thing else I can think of is that school starts in four weeks, and that's worse than poison ivy.

The stores already have signs in their windows saying "Back To School"—as if that was something to celebrate—and the child-size dummies are wearing sweaters, and flannel shirts, and corduroy knickers that squeak when you walk. Even the five-and-ten has back-to-school windows with composition books, pencils and erasers, book bags, ink bottles and pens. I wonder if anybody ever bought those red buttons I put back?

I'm still itchy, itchy, itchy!

If I have to get poison ivy, why can't it be after school starts? At least then I'd have an excuse to stay home for a few days.

I can't go swimming, and I can't play in the woods, and I'm not supposed to scratch, so I'm making a model airplane my mother bought me to keep my mind off how itchy my whole face is.

I'm making the model airplane on the dining-room table because there's lots of room to spread out. The framework of the plane's body and wings are finished and it looks pretty good—I followed the diagram very carefully. I've got airplane glue on my fingers, which doesn't wash off with soap. It's kind of fun to peel it off while I'm listening to the radio. All I have to do is glue the paper over the framework and the airplane will be finished. It's going to look nice.

My mother is listening to the radio in the kitchen, and it's almost three thirty, so I'm going up to my room to listen to *Jack Armstrong.*

"Ma, is it O.K. if I leave this here? I'll finish it later."

"O.K.," my mother says from the kitchen, "but you'd better put it away before your father comes home."

I go upstairs and listen to *Jack Armstrong* and *Captain Midnight* and *Little Orphan Annie.* Annie gives a secret message in code that you need her decoder ring to decipher. I had to send twenty-five cents and a label from Ovaltine to get the ring. Then I look at some of my *Jungle Comics* comic books. It sure is hot today. Jungle hot.

I look out the window and see Dukie sitting under the tree. He's panting. His water bowl is right near him and it looks O.K. for now. I have to keep refilling it because he keeps accidentally knocking it over.

Squeak! Bang!

I hear the screen door open and slam shut.

"I'm home, Ma!" Angel yells.

"Hang your wet suit on the line!" my mother yells.

"Angel!" I yell downstairs. "Don't touch anything on the dining-room table!"

My mother and Angel are talking in the kitchen but I can't make out what they're saying. *I'm having another itching attack.*

"Don't be late for dinner," I hear my mother say. "And don't slam the door!"

Squeak! Bang!

I go into the bathroom and put some more calamine lotion on my face. That stuff makes you look like a monster even if your face isn't swollen, but it stops the itch for about five minutes.

I hear my mother starting dinner so my father should be home soon with the funnies.

Squeak! Bang!

"Angel?" my mother yells from the kitchen.

"It's me," my father says, and his voice sounds funny.

It's funny that he slammed the screen door, too.

"Boy, it's hot," I hear my father say. "What are you making, Rose?"

"Steak."

"Ninety degrees—steak."

"You don't like it?" my mother says. "Eat salad."

"Rose," my father says, "why do you light the stove in this heat? You make the whole house hot."

"Don't start," my mother says. "What do you want from me? I try to make something different once in a while, or do you want us to just eat salad every night?"

"Ninety degrees—steak!" my father says, and

he starts cursing in Albanèse.

He's mad.

"Where are the children?" he asks my mother.

"Eddie's upstairs," my mother says, "and Angel isn't home yet."

"Where is he?"

"How should I know? You're his father—ask him when he comes home."

"He should be home," my father says. "What's burning?"

I hear the broiler tray being pulled out.

"Some of the grease caught fire," my mother says. "It's out."

"Ninety degrees—steak!" my father says again. "How are we going to eat in all this smoke?"

"We'll eat in the dining room," my mother says. "Eddie! We're ready to eat! Where is that Angel?"

"How can we eat in the dining room?" my father says. "The table isn't clean."

I hear my father cursing so fast it sounds like one word about a mile long. Then I hear some sounds but I can't tell what they are. One of them could be paper tearing.

"Mario!" my mother yells. "What did you do? The poor kid worked so hard all afternoon, and he isn't feeling well."

"They should play in the playroom!" my father yells.

Squeak! Bang!

All of a sudden it's very quiet, and I come downstairs kind of slowly because I'm afraid I might get yelled at for leaving the model airplane on the dining-room table. When I get to the bottom of the stairs, I see my mother kneeling on the dining-room floor picking up my model airplane that's in about a million pieces.

"Your father is in a lovely mood tonight," my mother says. "You shouldn't have left this on the table."

My throat feels tight, and I think I'm going to cry, so I run back up to my room and slam the door. Tears are running down my cheeks, and funny sounds are coming from my throat, and my face feels hot and that makes the poison ivy itch.

"Where were you?" I hear my father yell outside. Angel must be home.

"Dinner is on the table!" my mother yells from the dining room. "Nobody wants to eat? That's the thanks I get."

Squeak! Bang!

"Come on," my mother says. "It's getting cold. Eddie! Come and eat!"

I'm not going down there, and they better not

97

come up here. I lock my door. I wish I *was* a monster. I'd go downstairs and eat the three of them for dinner. I hear my father ask my mother something in Albanèse, and she answers in Albanèse. I wish they would talk English!

"Eddie!" my father yells upstairs. "Come and eat! Papa's sorry."

Grown-ups must think kids are really stupid. They do something real mean and then five minutes later we're supposed to forget all about it and act like nothing happened.

There's a knock on my bedroom door.

"Eddie," my father says through the door. "Come on, big boy. Dinner is on the table. I'll buy you another airplane."

I'm not even going to answer him.

"Papa's sorry," he says, and he tries to open my door. "It was hot downtown today, and I was busy and things went wrong at work, and the train was crowded. I was in a bad mood when I came home."

"If you had poison ivy," I say to myself, "you'd really be in a bad mood."

"Eddie," my father says, "open the door. Come and eat something, and after dinner we'll go to the movies. The air conditioning will feel good."

I might go to the movies just to get cool, but

I'm not talking to him, and I don't want another model airplane. I unlock my door but I don't open it. My father opens it and comes in.

"Let me see," my father says, and he tilts my head back to look at my face. "How do you feel?"

"Itchy."

When I get to the dining room Angel is all alone at the table eating steak with lots of ketchup, and on the table there's a big bowl of tomato-and-green-pepper salad, and a loaf of bread, and a pitcher of ice water.

"Sit down," my mother says from the kitchen. "I'm making you noodles with butter. The steak is cold, and you probably couldn't chew it anyway, with your poison ivy."

As I pass Angel I whisper, "We're going to the movies."

My father comes in and sits at the table.

"Rose," he says, "What do you say we go to the movies?"

"At least," my mother says, "we'll be cool for a couple of hours."

"What do you say?" my father says to Angel.

"Sure."

The noodles with butter tastes good—my mother put grated cheese and black pepper on top—and the salad is good, too. After dinner my mother puts the dishes in the sink and dabs some more calamine lotion on my face, and we all get in the car and drive down to the Central Theatre.

There's a sign on the box office that says "Healthfully Air Conditioned" and a picture of a polar bear. People are looking at me funny. If there was a Frankenstein picture playing they'd probably think I was the star, and ask for my autograph.

It's cold inside the theater and it feels good, but my mother brought sweaters just in case. I want to sit in the first row but my father says that's too close.

The main feature is a Betty Grable picture in technicolor. It's pretty to look at but the story is a lot like the last Betty Grable picture I saw. It will still be playing on Saturday so I'll be seeing it again.

When we come outside after the show, the streets are wet and a cool breeze is blowing.

"I left the windows open," my mother says. "I hope it didn't rain in. Is Dukie outside?"

"I took him in," Angel says.

I'm tired now and on the way home I fall asleep in the back seat. The next thing I know my father is carrying me up the stairs to my bedroom. He puts me on the bed and kisses my ear.

"Good night," he says.

I'm too sleepy to even answer. Then my mother undresses me— it tickles when she takes my socks off—and puts my pajamas on me. She puts just a sheet over me, and turns out the light.

"Good night," she says.

Just before I fall asleep I remember to pull up the legs of my pajama pants.

ten
RECITAL

I'm sitting on the front steps waiting for the Good Humor man and Dukie is with me. He doesn't have to be tied up anymore because we have a new mailman who isn't afraid of dogs. Dukie likes him. I look up the street for the Good Humor truck. All I see is those Egan kids in front of their house. School starts in two weeks and I'm not looking forward to it. But I'm glad I won't have Miss Sleeper anymore. Before I handed in my school books last June I erased the picture I drew of her in my English book. (It's a good thing I drew it in pencil.) Miss Sleeper probably checked every page of every book to make sure nobody marked them up.

In a little while my mother and Angel and I are going to Madam Marchisio's house. We have to take the trolley.

At the end of the summer Madam Marchisio gives a recital and invites her students' parents, and each student plays a special piece. The piece I'm going to play is "La Donna è Mobile." It's from an opera, and my father likes to hear me practice it. I'm scared because I have to play it in front of a lot of people. My father has to work today—even though it's Saturday—so he can't come.

Last Saturday I saw a movie about a concert pianist. There was a lot of piano playing in the movie and it made me want to practice and play good. I've been practicing "La Donna è Mobile" every day and pretending that I'm playing it in a movie.

A big, black car is coming down the street.

"Dukie, stay!"

The car passes and Dukie doesn't move.

"Good boy." And I pat his head and scratch him behind his ears. He would have chased that car if I hadn't been here to say "Stay!"

That car didn't belong to anybody around here. I wonder if it could have been a talent scout. All the movie studios have talent scouts who just travel around the country all the time looking for people who could become movie stars. If a talent scout ever did drive down this street he probably would discover those Egan kids.

The Good Humor man is late today. I hate waiting for people.

I go up and sit on the front porch. The French doors are open and I can see my reflection in a pane of glass. I can see the little blue scar under my left eye where the scissors hit me. I'll be ten years old in November but except for being taller I don't look any older than I did last year. Pretty soon I'll have to start paying fifty cents at the Central or have Angel buy my ticket for me.

In the movie last Saturday the actors were young at the beginning of the picture and got made up to look old at the end of the picture. I wonder how I'll look when I get old. I'll bet I can make myself look old.

I go inside and get the bottle of white shoe polish. Then I borrow an eyebrow pencil from my mother's dressing table—she'll get mad if she finds out.

I go into my room and close the door.

I dip my comb in the white shoe polish and comb it through my hair until my hair is all white. Then I carefully sharpen the eyebrow pencil and draw wrinkles around my eyes, and around my mouth, and on my forehead.

I get a tie out of my father's closet and put it on. It's one he doesn't wear much. Way in the back of his closet is an old jacket he never wears. I put it on, and in the pocket I find an old pair of his eyeglasses. Everything is blurry when I look through the eyeglasses, so I put them halfway down on my nose and look over them the way some old men do.

I look at myself in the mirror on the back of my door and I really look like an old man. I'll bet I could fool somebody.

When I go out the front door Dukie wags his tail and jumps on me. I can't fool him.

I go across the street to Mrs. D'Andrea's house and ring the bell. When she opens the door I'm all hunched over, and I say in a shaky, old-sounding voice, "'scuse me, lady . . ."

"Hello, Eddie," Mrs. D'Andrea says.

"Hello," I say.

"Aren't you warm in that jacket?" she says.

"No." But I really am.

"Eddie!" My mother is calling me.

"I have to go, Mrs. D'Andrea."

"Good-bye, Eddie." She's laughing.

"What have you got on your hair?" my mother says.

"Shoe polish."

"Shoe polish? What next? And look at your face."

"I'm pretending to be old," I say.

"I don't have to pretend," my mother says. "You're giving me gray hairs. Go upstairs and take a shower. We have to leave soon."

"Are you practicing for Halloween?" Angel says when I pass his room.

"It would make a good costume but I have to wash it off." And I go into the bathroom and take a shower.

"Come on!" my mother yells upstairs. "We're

going to be late."

I have on white pants, and brown-and-white shoes, and my sports shirt, with the palm trees on it, that I got for Christmas. My hair is still a little wet.

"Now you look nice," my mother says.

When we get outside, the Good Humor truck is in front of the Egan house.

"Look, Ma, the Good Humor man," Angel says.

"We don't have time," she says.

"We could eat it on the way," I say.

"In this heat?" my mother says. "You'll get it all over yourselves. And how can you play the piano with sticky fingers?"

The Egan kids are all eating Good Humors and grinning. There's ice cream all over their mouths.

We have to run to catch the trolley. Angel and I get to the corner first, and the trolley-car conductor sees us. We get on the trolley and wait for my mother. She's all out of breath when she gets on, and pays the fare.

"Thank you for waiting," she says to the conductor.

He rings the bell and starts the trolley, and we're on our way to Madam Marchisio's house.

It's very hot this afternoon, but Madam Marchisio's house looks cool under the big shade tree growing in her front yard.

Dickie and his mother are at the recital. There are also a lot of kids I don't know, their mothers, and a few fathers. It's hot inside the house, and Madam Marchisio serves hot tea.

"Hot drinks," she says, "make one feel cooler in warm weather."

I don't like tea but I'm even more scared now that I see all these strangers, so I drink some tea and it burns my tongue. I wish I had a Good Humor. I sit with my mother and Angel—he wants to take piano lessons, too—and wait for Madam Marchisio to call on me. I hope she doesn't call on me first.

"May I have your attention," Madam Marchisio says.

She is standing next to her black baby-grand piano, in front of her bay window, on a platform two steps above the rest of her living room. It's the first time I've seen her without a hat.

"I'm happy that you all could come this afternoon," she says, "so without further ado we shall have music. First, I'm pleased to introduce to you Irma Greener playing 'Come Back to Sorrento.'"

Everybody claps.

"I'm glad it's not me," I think. "But will I be next?"

107

When Irma Greener finishes her piece she stands up and curtsies, and everybody claps again.

"Very good, Irma," Madam Marchisio says. "And now we will hear Billy Taylor play 'The Toreador Song.'"

Everybody claps.

I hardly even hear what the other kids are playing. All I keep thinking is "Will I be next? Will I be next?" I still have a spot of poison ivy on my arm and it's starting to itch. I wish I was at the movies like every other Saturday afternoon. Everybody is clapping again so Billy Taylor must be finished.

"Thank you, Billy," Madam Marchisio says. "That was excellent. Next, Miss Shirley Hermann playing 'The Song of India.'"

Shirley's mother starts to clap ahead of everybody else. Shirley is fat, and she has on a yellow dress, and her face turns red when she sits at the piano. I know just how she feels. Now I wish I had been called on first because then I wouldn't still be scared.

"Sit up straight," my mother whispers to me.

When Shirley stands up after playing "The Song of India," her dress is stuck to her behind. Shirley's mother is still clapping even after everybody else has stopped, but Shirley doesn't curtsy before she goes back to her seat. Her mother pats Shirley's hand, and smooths the hair back off Shirley's forehead.

". . . And he will play 'La Donna è Mobile,' " Madam Marchisio is saying.

Angel pokes me in the arm. I didn't even hear Madam Marchisio call my name.

"Good luck," my mother whispers.

Everybody is clapping, and my stomach just did a somersault.

I feel like everybody is looking at me. I stand up and my arms feel about nine feet long, and my heart is pounding, and my hands are sweating. Now I know everybody is looking at me. All the way to the piano I keep my eyes on Madam Marchisio's carpet, and the room is very quiet just like the Reptile House at the zoo.

There isn't any carpet on the platform, and I hear my leather heels go *click! click! click!*

Squeak! When I sit on the piano bench one of its legs drags along the floor. I start playing my piece.

The beginning sounds pretty good but there's a hard part in the middle where I usually make a mistake, and now I'm really scared because that's the part I'm coming to. My heart feels like it's going to pop out of my ears. Here's the hard part. I play it perfectly.

I finish my piece, and everybody claps. I feel like taking a bow but I don't.

"That was beautiful, Eddie," Madam Marchisio says. "Thank you."

"Very good," my mother says when I get back to my seat.

Playing the piano for all these people was probably the scariest thing I ever did, but my face didn't turn red. Then some other kids play and

some of them make mistakes.

The last one to play is Dickie, and he doesn't look scared at all. His piece is a polonaise by Frederic Chopin, and it sounds beautiful. When he finishes, everybody claps longer than they did for anybody else, and Dickie bows and smiles. His mother claps the loudest, and when he goes back to his seat she smiles and kisses him. He really was the best one.

111

Now that the recital is over, Madam Marchisio gives out prizes. There are three categories: First Year, Second Year, and Third Year. In each category there's a first, second, and third prize. Nine kids are in the recital, so everybody gets a prize. I win second prize in the First Year. It's a little gold tie pin that looks like a harp but Madam Marchisio calls it a lyre. It's nice.

"May I have your attention please," Madam Marchisio says. "I now have a special treat for you. Minnie is going to sing."

Minnie is Madam Marchisio's old German shepherd. She sleeps on one of the twin beds in Madam Marchisio's bedroom.

"Sing, Minnie," Madam Marchisio says, and she sits at the piano and starts playing "Beautiful Dreamer."

"Beooootiful dreamer," Madam Marchisio sings, "wake unto meeeee."

Minnie is wagging her tail and looking up at Madam Marchisio.

"Sing, Minnie dear."

Minnie looks hot and tired. She sits on the floor, raises her head, and howls. Everybody laughs.

Minnie howls through the rest of "Beautiful Dreamer," and when it's over everybody claps. Minnie wins a prize, too. Madam Marchisio puts a dog biscuit inside a paper bag and ties the top of the bag closed.

"Here girl. Here, Minnie darling."

Minnie holds the bag between her paws and tears it open with her teeth. Then she eats the dog biscuit, wagging her tail.

On the trolley ride home I think, "I'm going to practice harder than ever and maybe at next year's recital I can play that polonaise."

My father is home when we get there.

"Pa, I won second prize."

"Good boy. Let me see."

The tie pin is in a little box with a cellophane top so I can show it without taking it out of the box. Then my father and I go downstairs, and I play 'La Donna è Mobile' for him just like I did at the recital. Dukie is downstairs listening, too, but he doesn't sing along.

"Very good!" my father says. "What would you like to do to celebrate?"

"Have a banana split at Howard Johnson's," I say. They have more flavors to pick from than Good Humor.

"O.K. Call Mama and Angel, and I'll get the car out."

"Ma! Angel! Come on! We're going to celebrate!"

And we all get in the car and drive down to

Howard Johnson's.

"Hello, dimples," the waitress says to Angel. She's the one we usually get. "What's this?" She's looking at the tie pin I stuck on my shirt collar.

"I won it for playing the piano."

"Congratulations. It isn't every day we get a celebrity in here. I wish I could play the piano but I'm all thumbs. Well, folks, what's your pleasure today?"

My father orders a black-and-white ice-cream soda, Angel orders a hot fudge sundae, my mother orders fruit salad because she's on a diet, and I order a banana split with three scoops—black raspberry, peach, and butter crunch.

It's a good celebration.

Format by Gloria Bressler
Set in 12 pt. Baskerville
Composed, and bound by The Haddon Craftsmen, Scranton, Pa.
Printed by The Murray Printing Company
HARPER & ROW, PUBLISHERS, INCORPORATED